# A Battleaxe and a Metal Arm 11:

# *The Laboratory of Mr. Mask*

Samuel Fleming

Cover Art by David Leahey

ISBN-13: 978-1-954679-31-3 (paperback)
ISBN-13: 978-1-954679-30-6 (ebook)

Thank you to my Beta Readers

and to my First Reader,

Mel.

iv

# Contents

"Those who hoped they
would find salvation in death
will find nothing of the sort."
—wavering

# Previously...

After waking in the dungeon for the first time, Helesys and Taunauk journeyed through the flooded realm of the fishmen. They met the unfortunate creature, Pitiful Lull, and rescued a water elemental by pulling a metal plate—the wolf-plate— from its watery body. Though they would perish by the maws of the giant hydra, they would be reborn again in the same hallway—or so they thought. The hall had changed, and they had returned with the wolf-plate.

They would learn in the second realm that bringing back treasure was a feat few others could claim. After fighting their way through the horde of goblins in the abandoned barracks and obsidian mechanical soldiers, the giant, Zhug, favored the heroes with wisdom and boons: The magekiller token and the ironwood shield, Everfall. It was also he who told them of the many lingering deaths that plagued the dungeon, one of which was the many-handed horror, Shomosk, whom they had narrowly avoided in Zhug's crypt!

Plagued by memories of blastshells and by Taunauk's mysterious golden glow, the pair wandered the realm of the Wode, a dark and sprawling forest. There they met many inhabitants, including the wolf druids, led by Matron Mildé, and the village ruled over by the Deacon. The Deacon's village was especially troubling, as the channeler used the flesh of his people to make things for them—tools, homes, even children. Helesys would come to despise these gods and demigods, who chose to rule and stagnate rather than escape. At the crumbling Gatehouse, they learned the story of the Gatekeeper and her Wolf-Knight, and that they held the keys to escaping the dungeon. Taunauk ultimately perished by the sword of the Green Knight, and Helesys would fall from the heights of the infinite wall.

In spite of their differing deaths, Helesys and Taunauk were reborn together again in the hallway—fated to always do so. They followed the tunnel underground, fighting through the denizens of the giant insect hive. In their wake, the heroes found human slaves of the hive, and freed them by death. The heroes would call on all their powers to defeat the spider-king and then to cross the underground chasm after. Ultimately, the strange glassmen would not aid them, and sent them wandering again.

Their fifth death saw them climb upwards, past hanging banners and carvings of wolves, and the first meeting with the mysterious rogue, Shawn—who would prove to be a formidable ally and friend. The wolf-plate from their first rebirth gained them entry to a greenhouse. There they found the remnants of a mages' battle and the Ring of Winter. Their path continued upward through an elevator filled with shades. Inside, Helesys was forced to use the holding spell on the horrific dancer—a feat that should've been impossible on such a dark-minded construct, and that Helesys would second guess long after they'd left. At the top of the tower, they eventually found the wizard, Amadeus. There they realized several things: That Amadeus recognized the Everfall shield and the aid of Zhug, that Shawn was like the heroes—he could bring back relics, and that the dungeon was a soul trap—a bottomless well from which souls cannot escape. But when questions turned to the Wolf-King and the Gatekeeper, Amadeus cowered. The Wolf-

King possessed him—in his own sanctum—and the heroes struggled to stand against his might. The three ultimately leapt from the wizard's tower, fell to their deaths and woke again… But Shawn was not with them. And yet, they felt they hadn't seen the last of him.

Next, their journey led them through a mist-covered jungle. They passed strange, enormous totems, and fought sinister cannibals and bonemen. Soon, they found the grotto of the serpent Irehyl, who directed them against the Apothecary. Underground, they found the Apothecary, defeated her and ceased the giant bonfire that the cannibals relied upon. In doing so, they changed the realm, and Helesys also learned how to pry apart the seams between worlds and walk between them without death.

Their journey took them across an endless beach, past a derelict castle home to two men who lived and squalor and surfed upon a magic shield. They came to the cursed ship, the Malorienta, run aground for supplies and ready to set sail. Their comrade, Shawn, was waiting for them, and the three set sail for the edge of the world. But the journey was perilous, and they narrowly survived a living reef, strange sirens, man-eating eels from the depths, and the Narrows. Among their discoveries was Pitiful Lull, whose mind and essence were split across the realms by an accident with its associate, the wizard Amadeus. The three comrades would ultimately perish in the storm at the end of the world, but would each wake separately on a strange beach. Helesys remembered her mother and her sister, and how she had left for the elven legion—that her long hair was an illusion, and was cut short for service. On the beach, an ambiguous voice addressed her by name, admitted to giving them the power to bring back artifacts after death, and beseeched her help to defeat the Wolf-King. Their task now was to use Zhug's aid to reach the depths of the ocean, and find The Machine of Antrikaumora.

Helesys and Taunauk woke underground, alone, and continued through ancient caverns to find the long-lost City of Shéslang. Helesys was able to open the city gates, but the pair found the entire city overwhelmed by the parasite, the Duoausongur—a lingering death first encountered in the realm of the fishmen. They used the jade lemur to fly high above the hellscape, gaining passage from the indigenous lemurs that lived in the upper passages, and barely surviving the psychic powers of the blue Terrans that lived deep in the walls. Upward they flew, to the ends of the tunnel, and found the shrunken remnant of the god serpent Shéslang. The serpent offered them knowledge, a boon, and a path: Knowledge of three brothers who once sought the Wolf-King and failed. A boon of a magic spear—the Gar of Shéslang. A path through a seam of the realms—to the realm of the Cogheart and then to the Godpeak. One-Mind would aid Helesys while the spirits atop the mountain would aid Taunauk.

In the realm of the Cogheart, they found Shawn waiting for them. He had learned from the voice on the beach that he was neither human nor elf—that his heritage was a mystery. Taunauk revealed that his exile was a mystery as well, since he was allowed to keep his heirloom axe. The trio journeyed together across the rocky wasteland, and were led underground by Porthmeus, a free automaton. The heroes journeyed into One-Mind's lair, first having to evade and best its automated defenses—swarms and vicious automatons. In the fray, Helesys felt Shawn's strange, wind-like powers, and Taunauk manifested three other glowing Endroggen warriors. Afterward, they would twice encounter the twisted hunter-killer abomination, Dissimul, before One-Mind let them come inside its core. Inside the core, they saw the druid grove that One-Mind called home until it was copied and imprisoned in a magic mirror. Eventually, that copy was trapped inside the dungeon. Dissimul and other automatons were also copies of One-Mind, ones that occasionally needed to be culled. Like the wizard, Amadeus, One-Mind also sought escape into a realm of its own making. One-Mind repaired Helesys's wand-arm, a connection that was severed before she was imprisoned.

But when they tried to journey to the Godpeak, Helesys, Taunauk, and Shawn were intercepted and trapped in a long, alien hallway—a trap meant to test their resilience. All the while, the strange captor scryed on them with a touch as subtle as Amadeus's.

It wasn't until they finally stopped to rest that the trap was sprung: Spider-like creatures stepped from the orange portals that lined the walls and unleashed psionic power against the heroes.

When they finally woke, they were imprisoned aboard an alien vessel—a living ship. Helesys woke to a voice in her head that revealed itself to be the wand embedded in her metal arm. It had been speaking subtly to her all along, but One-Mind's repairs let it directly talk to her. Helesys freed herself from both her confines and the slug in her head, then helped Taunauk and Shawn to do the same.

The heroes crept through the vessel and found a spawning pool for the blue-veined slugs and a green portal holding the memories of one of the alien creatures. Helesys saw the life of the Idnauthi, a race of parasitic, squid-like creatures from the stars. A slug would implant in a host's brain, take over their mind and body, then grow into an adult Idnauthi. The iihdii was the Idnauthi word for where a host went when the slug took over its mind… and it was the same word they used for the dungeon. Most Idnauthi were asleep, ready to journey back to the stars from whence they came.

Lastly, Helesys saw the memory of the living ship as it soared through the blackness of space. No other creature could recall what the dungeon looked like before they were imprisoned, but through the ship, Helesys saw it—a bulbous, writhing cloud that moved as if it were alive. Her mind was filled with an overwhelming, singular, desperate voice even greater than the Duoausongur, and Helesys felt fear unlike anything she had ever felt before.

Only moments had passed while Helesys saw these events through their enemy's eyes, but it was enough to alert the scrying alien to their presence. Other enslaved Terrans woke, but Helesys was able to free them with the blight spell. But as the slugs left their ears, the heroes and the newly freed Terrans still weren't safe—

The scrying Idnauthi, Sigun, used overwhelming psionic power to hold their bodies in place. While it boasted, Helesys was able to find the source of its immense power—the living ship was a conduit and was bolstering Sigun's power. With her magekiller token, Helesys severed the connection, and the heroes were able to chase Sigun away.

As it fled, Sigun called upon the Rithdai, a hulking mix of eagle, bear, and Idnauthi. Shawn fled with the freed Terrans to search for an escape, while Helesys and Taunauk fought the powerful creature. In the end, it took ice to weaken its armored hide and the might of Helesys's spear and Taunauk and his golden warriors to defeat it.

The pair caught up to the others, and Helesys used her wand to blow open a hole in the living ship. From there, they leapt down to the roof of the castle and crawled through another hole into the attic. Then Helesys reached out to the arcane engines of the ship and activated them, hurling it into up into the sky.

The group journeyed down into the attic, a massive opening lined with bodies of the dead and preserved. Helesys used her warding light to keep away the blank-faced Terrans that creeped at the edge of their vision. As they walked, Helesys confided in the group of her wand speaking to her, and Taunauk confided that his Endroggen spirits spoke little.

Just when it seemed that they had escaped the alien grasp of the Idnauthi, the snarling visage of Sigun attacked them. The alien had been sucked through the hole in the ship and sought revenge. In the end, Helesys struggled to hold both the warding light and defend herself against Sigun. In the end, Helesys relinquished her light and bolstered Shawn, who vanished and attacked Sigun. When the warding light faded, the injured Idnauthi was snatched by the blank-faced Terrans and dragged away into the darkness. Meanwhile, Shawn radiated mist.

Helesys kindled light, pushing away the blank-faded Terrans, and holding tight to the young ones they freed.

~ ~ ~

# Desolation

Helesys led them farther into the cavernous attic of the castle, her gauntlet held high above her head and burning with warding light.

Though they had no concept of time in the indoor space, Helesys knew that they had already walked for an entire day. There seemed no end to the attic. The floor beneath her feet was packed tight with the bodies of the mummified dead, their colorful clothes extending out like a patchwork quilt. They creaked beneath her like a rickety, carpeted floor. Thick vertical beams rose through the bodies and to the ceiling one hundred feet above. There, the trusses of the castle roof extended out into the gloom, their slope so slight that Helesys couldn't tell which direction it ran.

Beside her walked the barbarian, Taunauk, and the rogue, Shawn, her familiar comrades. Just behind them were the surviving Terrans from the Idnauthi ship—the aliens that had pulled them into this godsforsaken end of the dungeon. The aliens that had nearly taken over their bodies, nearly trapping them in a prison within a prison.

Helesys winced at the memories. She had seen much through the stored memories of the Idnauthi ship—much that she wished she could unsee.

And she winced at the soreness that had seeped into every inch of her muscles, bones, and even burned dully in her metal arm—

At the edge of the light, creatures stood, walked, and watched. Terran in shape only. Their eyes white, their faces smudged into blurry approximations. Even the clothes on their bodies were blurred so that the lines between skin and their clothing were indistinguishable.

Helesys had burned the warding light since they set foot in the attic and would continue to burn it because it was the only thing that kept the creatures at bay.

She'd been afraid to sleep at first, afraid that she would lose the spell, that in the moments it would take to wake her the creatures would close in around them and carry off one of her comrades or one of the freed Terrans that depended on them. Turn them into one more of the blank faces that lurked at the edge of the light.

She had already seen the creatures carry away one of the Idnauthi. Sigun—the alien that had fallen from the ship—came for them in the attic. Nearly bested Helesys, Taunauk, and Shawn at the same time. Even with all that power, when the light fell, the blank-faced Terrans carried Sigun off into the darkness and the poor bastard couldn't even scream.

Sometimes at the edge of the light, Helesys would see the smudged form of the alien lurking with the other creatures. The powerful visage of the alien reduced to a child's painting—mute and smudged—and all the more terrifying for what it symbolized.

Half a dozen lives ago, the giant, Zhug, had said that there were gods trapped here in the dungeon, and that there were things that even the gods feared. He warned the heroes of the many lingering deaths that awaited them. Helesys had believed his words, but she still shivered at the thought of just how many lingering deaths they had already seen.

No—Helesys wouldn't allow such a fate to befall them. Not to those that trusted her or those that depended on her.

But her wand insisted that she sleep. Taunauk and Shawn insisted too. So, for a few restless hours, Helesys had slept on the patchwork floor, her gauntlet locked so that it stood up in the air, warding light holding back the denizens of the attic and her comrades huddled around her like a campfire.

The rest of the time, she kindled strength and light. Body aching despite the magical reinforcement. Even the Gar of Shéslang was little help—its power seemed fit only for battle and strife, not for the droll of survival. The spear that had pierced the hide of a god, now merely steadied Helesys's gait like a walking stick.

Back in the early days, when Helesys and Taunauk had wandered in the enormous forest of the wode… She'd walked by herself for three days and three nights to reach the infinite wall. What strength did she have then that she lacked now? Was it because she'd only died twice before the wode? …Only failed twice? Or was it that now she'd had the hope, the confidence—the arrogance—beaten out of her?

No—she *tried* to tell herself that it was because death was a release, that each time they died, their food and strength were refreshed and reset. Now, they'd already wandered through the caverns of the serpent Shéslang, through the underground realm of the Cogheart, then captured by the Idnauthi and subsequently broken free—already three realms of strife with little pause and no rest.

Yet it didn't matter. There was no rest or peace to be had in the attic. There had to be somewhere else.

Shawn walked beside her and whispered, "I think we're getting closer." The rogue held a simple coin in his hand—supposedly a magical coin.

Taunauk grumbled, "You said that thing only guided you to drink."

Shawn nodded. "And that must be better than here."

"...Last time the tavern tried to eat you."

From behind them, one of the survivors, Richard, grumbled, "I don't want to be eaten," eliciting several more mumbles from the group of rescued Terrans.

One of which, being Scarlett, the red-haired elven girl, calm beyond her years, who replied, "There, there, Richard."

"Nevermind that," Shawn said. "The point is, it's somewhere different."

Helesys too felt the familiar pull of guidance from her wand-arm. "Shawn's right," the weaver said. "I feel it too."

*Not much further*, her wand-arm said, always speaking internally. It's voice was smooth and neither male nor female—reminiscent of the automatons from One-Mind's realm.

Shawn raised an eyebrow. "Feel it *or hear it?*"

The elf chuckled wearily. "My wand actually hasn't spoken much to me since we escaped."

*There's been more pressing concerns, like keeping your gauntlet lit.*

Helesys shook her head at the internal interruption. "What about you, Taunauk? Have you heard more from the spirits?"

"No," Taunauk replied. The barbarian scanned the unchanging landscape at the edge of the light; the only hint to his fatigue were the dark circles under his eyes.

Helesys turned to the rogue. "What about you? Have you given any more thought to your wispy powers?"

Shawn smiled nervously, his mouth almost hanging open, as if he were wondering what not to say instead.

"You don't have to tell us," she added, watching his reaction.

Shawn shut his thin lips and shook his head. "It's not that. I… I just don't understand it. If I'm supposedly different, then why are my only memories of working in a factory… beside humans? If I was an air elemental, shouldn't I have memories of—I don't know, *flying*, or something?"

"It takes time," said the young voice from behind them. Scarlett jogged up to them. "I still remember things. Even now."

Shawn peered down at her. "And just how long have you been here?"

"Some forty years," said another behind them. Isabella, the young girl's adopted elven mother. Unlike her daughter, Isabella wasn't as forthcoming with knowledge or aid.

Shawn blinked his eyes. "I should hope I look so young for forty."

"Are you part elf?" Scarlett asked. "Even the half breeds live a long time." The rogue chuckled at that.

Helesys turned to the young elf. "Scarlett, where did you and your family live?"

Scarlett looked back quickly to get her mother's approval before answering, "The Frozen Isles."

"Was it a big place?"

The girl shook her head. "It was Lesthem. A fishing village. Why do you ask?"

Helesys shook her head and forced a smile. "I don't remember much, but I think I lived in an elven city. A great big one."

"The only one," Isabella said. And when Helesys slowed, the elven woman stepped forward and walked beside them. "Novissimé is the *only* elven city. They live apart from the world, spending their lives researching magic, technology, and fighting in The Eternal War."

Simultaneously, images and questions swirled in Helesys's mind: Images of an immense, towering city set between the mountains in the far reaches of the real world—so large that it spanned the peaks between two mountains and rose nearly as high. Elves walked the streets beside clockwork automatons, a whole city kept clean and unmarred by magic that was imbued in every stone block. A city of wonders and limitless magic, yet... the populace hung under the threat of ever present war—*The Eternal War.*

Questions came that hadn't even occurred to Helesys to ask, for when one has no knowledge at all, they have no questions from which to start. Such broad questions yielded nothing but short and uninteresting answers.

Finally, Helesys asked the question that formed a pit in her stomach. "What is the Eternal War?"

Isabella looked to her daughter and wrapped an arm around Scarlett's shoulders. "Hundreds of years ago, after the elders retreated behind the city walls, they wanted a place where they could practice warfare... in case the humans or any other should come for Novissimé. So they opened a portal to another dimension.

"Inside, they tested their war machines and destructive magic. Since the damage was in this other world, they didn't have to worry about the repercussions.

"Then one day, the Shadowkind appeared. They say they look like us. That they can shape their hands into weapons and conjure things from the shadows—that they are as innumerable as night.

"Ever since, Novissimé and the Shadowkind have been at war. Even with all their magic, Novissimé can't win. Everything goes toward the war."

Helesys nodded as the words rang true. "What of the Houses?"

"What of them?" Isabella scoffed. "The nobles are the ones that continue, that hoard and funnel all our resources toward the war. Our children… That's why we left, why most elves leave. My family were humble tradespeople. We did not want to be a part of it anymore."

Helesys's gaze fell shamefully to the patchwork floor. "I am sorry. Merely curious. We should keep going."

But before she could turn, Isabella reached for her sleeve. The elf glanced at Helesys's arm. "Perhaps I spoke too harshly. Were you a soldier?"

"I think so," Helesys replied, forcing a smile. "Trying to get from one battlefield to another. Come, let's save the rest of our conversation for a better place."

The weaver turned and flared her gauntlet's light a little brighter, eager to be done with the conversation. Meanwhile, Taunauk and Shawn both glanced at her with concern written on their faces.

Helesys let her half-truth about being a soldier drift life-lessly through the air and imagined it settling somewhere alongside the fleeting joy she'd felt at remembering her home. It didn't much matter where she came from or what she was—soldier, noble, heir of a great house—if they didn't make it out of this damned place.

~

When the survivors grew weary, they stopped to camp for the second time.

Sleep was fitful for all. It was a grisly thing—sleeping on the mummified backs that lined the floor. Everyone slept on their backs, facing the rafters, so that they could pretend the floor beneath them was normal.

Staying up on watch was worse, for the blank-faced Terrans always stood just at the edge of the light. Occasionally, one would scurry around to stand somewhere else—always too fast to be seen.

Helesys would try not to look directly at the creatures, try not to acknowledge them, because now and then she would look out and find the smudged form of Sigun staring back.

Helesys woke Shawn for the next watch, and the rogue shuddered at her touch.

"Sorry," he said groggily. "Can't wait to be out of this place. I think we're close."

The weaver smiled, whispering, "Did your coin tell you that?"

"In a fashion." Shawn followed her gaze across the attic to Sigun. "Serves the bastard right. Thanks for freeing me, by the way, when he came for us."

Helesys nodded. "It seemed like the best course. I know you're still figuring out yourself, but you've got a knack for resisting assaults on the mind—be them magical or psychic."

"And I'm getting better. I don't like to be made a fool twice." Shawn nodded reluctantly. "Should've figured you would pick up on that. Not much gets past you."

"You sound disappointed."

The rogue met her eyes, and something flashed across his face that Helesys couldn't make out: Mischievousness or reluctance, or mistrust. Then it was gone, and Shawn picked idly at his fingernails.

"I was just wondering if we should be sharing *everything* we remember with one another."

"I... I had similar thoughts," she replied. "But I don't feel that way now."

Shawn eyed her now. "What about that theory that we were tracking someone or running from someone?"

"It's just a theory."

"What if you and Taunauk were tracking me?" After Shawn said it, he couldn't meet her eyes. "It would explain it, right? You were following me... and I got caught by the dungeon just a little before you and Taunauk. I'm different, right? Everybody sees it. Maybe that's why you were after me."

Helesys's face softened, and she waved her glowing metal fingers. "We're all a little different. Do you really believe that?"

Shawn shrugged, then gestured around. "We've had nothing but time to think since we've been here. It's hard to shake."

The weaver shook her head. "I don't believe that's the reason. You feel too familiar to be our enemy."

The rogue nodded slightly, then cracked a smile. "I'll give you that. That would be a pretty crappy twist. What's it matter, anyway? We're still trapped. Can't take me to elf jail if we're in the bottom of the *smiihdii*."

Helesys shook her head. "It was the *iihdii*."

Shawn waved a hand. "One man's *iihdii* is another man's *smiihdii*. Get some sleep."

Helesys laid down, still shaking her head at the absurdity, her wand-arm locked so that it stood up like a lantern. She tried not to think about the uneven floor at her back. Then she closed her eyes and turned her thoughts inward.

Helesys said internally to her wand, *You've been as quiet as Taunauk.*

*I am still here, Helesys of Great House Byyra. We communicate often without words. It is quicker that way.*

*…So you said. Do you remember anything else about the Novissimé or about our life before?*

*Our life?*

Helesys's eyebrows wrinkled at that. *Yes. I assumed we'd been together for some time. Do you remember otherwise?*

*I am still remembering, though your conversation with Isabella helped. What she said of the city of Novissimé and about the Eternal War are correct. Few elves emigrate elsewhere, though; the rate was perhaps one in two thousand.*

*What of us?* Helesys asked. *Isabella has seen my gauntlet. Even though she was a tradeswoman, it didn't seem strange. Were amputations and prosthetics common?*

*Yes. Novissimé was at the pinnacle of magic, clockwork, and automatons. Smaller machines labored around the city. Larger ones were embedded in buildings. Gauntlets such as your arm would've been common for injuries. Though I think your Great House afforded you the best of technology.*

Helesys smirked and asked in jest, *So not everyone spoke to their wands as I do?*

*No.*

The weaver's smile faded. *Is it common for nobles to fight in the war like I did?*

*…Yes.*

*Why do you hesitate?*

*I am sorry, Helesys. It is strange to know some things and not others. It is common for nobles to command and even fight in the Eternal War. But injuries do not seem common.*

*What about the Shadowkind?*

*I am sorry, Helesys. I do not remember.*

Frustrated, the weaver asked, *What of other Terrans? Do they fight beside us?*

*No. Other Terrans are not allowed in the city walls. Only elves fight in the Eternal War. And… emigrants are sworn to secrecy as a condition of their leaving. Sworn never to speak of it.*

Helesys's thoughts drifted off, dwelling on the new information.

She was a member of Great House Byyra and also involved in the Eternal War. Then Injured and given the best of prosthesis. Then sent away from the battlefield and outside the walls of the city. And for some reason, journeyed alongside an Endroggen barbarian and a strange rogue before they were trapped in the dungeon.

Helesys opened her eyes and squinted to look at her glowing gauntlet. To be given such a powerful weapon, and then be sent away from the battlefield… And then there was what One-Mind said when it repaired the connection in her wand-arm, the same one that now allowed Helesys to speak with her wand—a connection "likely severed before you were trapped here" and that kept her powers from their full potential…

Frustration and anger simmered in the elf, and she pushed them aside. She needed to rest. She had the rest of her life to dwell on thoughts of sabotage. They would do her no good at present.

~

The next time they woke, Helesys led them across the attic for several more hours—

Until they came to a slope on the floor. At first, the slope was gentle, but as they walked to the edge of it, they saw a huge pit in the distance.

Tentatively, they descended toward it.

The pit stretched out across the attic, nearly spanning the breadth of the warning light that Helesys kept burning. The gentle slope was gone, replaced with Terran-sized steps that descended down some hundred feet.

And at the center of the pit was an opening—a square cut-away through which green light shone.

The strange image occurred to Helesys that bodies had been brought through the hatch and subsequently dumped in the attic—in an ever-increasing pile. She shivered at the thought.

Shawn whispered, "I think that's where we need to go. That's where my coin is pointing toward."

Helesys nodded. Her wand guided her similarly. She moved to go first and lead them, but Taunauk stopped her.

The barbarian pointed back the way they came, to the blank-faced Terrans that mulled at the edge of the light. "I will go first."

All Helesys could do was watch as Taunauk crept down the steps of mummified bodies, axe and Everfall shield in hand.

Her gaze flitted between him and the outer reaches of the attic, where dozens of creatures stood, where Sigun's blurry form stood. Helesys grit her teeth and flared her warding light a little brighter.

Taunauk reached the opening. The furs of his cloak glowed a bright green in the light. First he peered through, looking carefully to either side. Then he lowered the butt of his axe through as if seeing if it was real or if it was a trap. Last, he let go of Everfall and reached his left arm through the opening.

The barbarian stood up, satisfied. "There are walkways. I will go first. The little ones will need help to get down."

With that, the group approached while Helesys stayed toward the top of the pit and kept her eyes on the attic.

One by one, the group jumped into the opening and Helesys took tentative steps to the bottom.

When everyone else was through, Helesys stepped to the edge of the opening and peered through. The rest of them stood on a metal catwalk suspended high in the air. The green glow came from somewhere below—somewhere impossibly distant.

Behind her, blank faces crouched just above the edge of the pit and peered at her like curious children.

Helesys motioned for the group to give her space, then dropped through the hole and landed with a bang on the catwalk. She looked out over the landscape.

The catwalk was a single sheet of metal about two persons wide with thin railings about hip height. It stretched off into the distance in either direction, disappearing into green mist at the farthest points. Below them, the cavern vanished into a green abyss. Whatever metal the catwalk and railings were made of must have been incredibly strong, for Helesys couldn't see any support beams or cables holding the catwalk up or holding the railings steady. They seemed to hang in the thick green air, along with a coppery taste, like lightning about to strike—the air of latent magic.

One of the rescued women screamed and pointed to the opening in the attic ceiling.

Blank-faced Terrans huddled around the opening, peeking over with just blurry eyes and foreheads.

Helesys ushered the group away from the opening. As they shuffled along the smooth metal of the catwalk, Helesys watched the attic opening carefully, but no creatures came through. Then the weaver slowly relaxed her warding light until it was overshadowed by the eerie green glow that permeated the room.

The creatures didn't come through, nor did they peer any further over the edge of the opening.

"The green light holds them at bay," Taunauk muttered.

"Good," Shawn added. "I'm not sure what's in store for us, but I'd rather fall to my death than whatever lingering death that was back there."

Helesys thought back to Sigun and the alien's lifeless face and shuddered. It was up there somewhere, likely huddled with other creatures around the attic opening. Was Sigun still in that lifeless face? Or was Sigun's mind gone and cast away somewhere? Or trapped in an iihdii—a prison?

When she was finally convinced that none of the creatures would follow, Helesys said, "Let's go."

"Which way?" the young Scarlett asked.

Helesys motioned along the catwalk in the other direction from the attic. Anywhere but there, she thought quietly.

~ ~ ~

# Catwalks and Vessels

The group walked on across the catwalk, their steps echoing dully on the metal. Shawn led the group, following the direction of his magic coin. Taunauk walked behind to guard their rear. Helesys walked in the middle with the freed Terrans, wand-arm hanging at her side. Though she often didn't feel pain or discomfort in the metal, now it felt half numb at her side from the days of constant use.

The heroes and survivors had walked for hours, yet found no end to the journey. Nor had they found any hanging struts or seems in the metal. Helesys could feel faint magic in the structure, but nothing that suggested a power that could hold up such a structure.

*It is an effect of time,* her wand said internally, answering her thought. *Over long times and repeated castings, magic can coalesce in material, be it weapon, wand, or structure. Wherever we are, it is immensely old.*

Sometime later, a set of a dozen glass tubes appeared. They hung in the air about twenty feet from the catwalk, each stretching from the mist below up into the ceiling above, and arranged side by side by increasing size. The smallest might have been the width of a sword, while the largest was twice as broad as Taunauk.

"What in Movernus's name are those for?" Shawn muttered.

"Do not give breath to fate," Taunauk replied sullenly.

"They lead to the attic," young Scarlett whispered.

And with her words, red liquid bubbled up through the smallest tube, turning from a trickle to a stream.

The group stood immobile on the catwalk, watching the silent procession in the glass. Green bile rose through another tube, yellow bubbling liquid through another, and finally clear liquid. Through the middle tubes rose various bones: Digits of fingers and toes. Chunks of vertebrae and finally arms, legs, ribs and a Terran skull. Organs came next according to size.

In the largest tube, clothes fluttered upward, like bright sheets billowing in the wind—a torn green shirt, gray trousers, and sections of pink skin. And as they rose, the few children in the group whimpered in horror.

"By Movernus," Shawn whispered. "What in purple Tamir have we—"

"Shawn," Taunauk said quietly. The barbarian gestured to the children, and Shawn took his meaning: They were scared enough as it was.

Helesys added, "Whoever trifles with us will not find easy prey. Come on." She ushered them forward across the catwalk.

The weaver did not want to dwell on it either. For every strange realm came new challenges… new monsters and new horrors.

Yet, there was something else: She was no expert in anatomy, but she recognized most things that had drifted up the tubes. Of all the parts and pieces, there were several missing. The bones seemed too few, and there were no muscles and no brain.

~

Hours later, the group came to an impasse.

At first, it seemed as if the catwalk abruptly ended, but as they approached, they saw that the hand rails turned and continued straight down.

Taunauk walked to the edge first and peered over. A moment later, he turned, frowned, and called for Helesys.

"What do you feel?" he asked.

The weaver looked over the edge. The catwalk didn't end—it followed the railing straight down into the glowing green abyss, as if it continued in that new direction. As she stared, it didn't feel as if the catwalk was supported in such a manner… Helesys opened her senses and felt the tenuous air of magic that followed the metal.

Helesys gripped the metal hand holds and leaned over, and her stomach began to turn—not at the dizzying height, but because she could feel the change in gravity. Slowly, the weaver leaned farther and farther over, kindling strength so that she could hold on to the railing should her assumption be wrong.

Someone behind her gasped, but the weaver paid them no mind.

Helesys didn't need to hold on nearly so tight, because her feet were firmly on the platform. When she was completely on the other side and staring down into the abyss, Helesys let go with one hand and finally the other, and she stayed stuck to the side.

For a moment, she could forget that she was facing downward. All her senses, even her muscles, were convinced that this new direction was forward, instead of down.

It was only when she looked back and saw Taunauk's curious expression that her stomach turned again.

"It's perfectly safe," Helesys said to Taunauk. "Gravity has been changed, that's all."

Shawn stayed at the back of the group, keeping watch. Taunauk ushered the survivors forward.

Little Scarlett volunteered to go first, taking tentative steps, before stumbling into Helesys's arms. The elven girl looked up with a smile.

"Very good," Helesys said. "Stand close."

One by one, Taunauk and Helesys helped the survivors transition to the downward catwalk. Some took to the change in gravity more smoothly than others. The few children were especially quick.

Taunauk and Shawn were last, both men with their difficulties.

Taunauk was hesitant, but took to the new direction quickly. He grumbled something about magic, but walked forward again to the head of the group.

Meanwhile, Shawn grimaced while inching forward. "There's something eerie about this," he said.

Helesys smirked. "What's eerie about standing on a vertical surface?"

Shawn inched forward until he was nearly done, then his face turned yellow. The rogue took the last step and leaned over the railing, vomiting into the abyss. Bile sprayed forward and then changed course to sail past the rest of the group—thankfully getting on no one.

The rogue wiped his mouth with his sleeve. "Sorry," he muttered.

Scarlett called from behind, "It's okay, Shawn!"

"It'll pass in a moment," Helesys offered.

Shawn still clung to the railing. He nodded, then shook his head, then nodded one final time.

~

Again their journey dragged on, until hours had passed, and Helesys had nearly forgotten that gravity had changed and they were walking down instead of forward.

From beyond the faint mist, the green glow grew even brighter, as if they were coming closer to the source of the light. As it grew closer, the mist began to swirl and churn. Sounds of splashing came next.

Soon the world grew so bright it felt as if they'd stepped into another realm—one where they were suspended in the midst of a lime green sky. A steady breeze came, bringing with it the pungent smell of copper and metal. Helesys mused that even the automaton realm of One-Mind hadn't smelled that strong. But there was something else too—disinfectant.

Helesys snapped back to the moment, because a large eel swam by them—coming from beneath the catwalk and swimming overhead toward the green—as if it were still on the original plane of gravity.

The weaver did a double take. The eel was some ten feet long and slender, with brilliant purple scales and fangs poking out from its lips.

Shawn pointed as it passed. "Does anyone else see that?" When no one dignified him with a response, the rogue peeked at the rest of them and sighed. "Thank Movernus for that."

"What's going on?" one of the survivors whispered.

After the eel passed, Taunauk reached out with Everfall as far as he could, swinging the battleaxe back and forth. Though mist wavered around the blade, it met no resistance. "It's like they're swimming through air," he said.

Helesys added, "And it seems like gravity only works to our benefit when we're close to the walkway."

Shawn chuckled. "Don't go jumping off. Got it."

They passed dozens of other strange aquatic creatures swimming through the mist: Enormous manta rays that seemed to radiate darkness instead of shadow. Schools of bright blue jellyfish and thousands of tiny silver fish no bigger than a finger. Then there were singular fish in an amalgamation of shapes, sizes, and fins—like they had been made by children rolling dice. Twice, great whales swam by, their flanks like walls of mottled gray flesh and their calls echoing through the metal of the catwalk.

As the heroes and survivors walked, Helesys breathed a sigh of relief that none of the creatures seemed to notice their presence, nor swim close to the path they walked.

Then they came upon a rocky formation that stretched as far as they could see across the mist. Frilled creatures speckled the surface and waved back and forth in an invisible current, like grass in a windblown field. There, life seemed even more abundant: Crabs walked over the rocks, their shells warped into even stranger shapes than the wondrous fish from above; some were bulbous and knobbed, others slender as disks, others as long as worms.

They followed the catwalk all the way to the rocks and through a tunnel that seemed to bore through the formation itself. They passed into eerie darkness and quiet, lit only by tiny formations of moss or algae, which smoldered with dull reds and greens, while the familiar green mist burned in the distance.

"What mess have we wandered into?" Shawn mused quietly.

Though they were at opposite ends of the group, Taunauk replied, "One that shall soon pass."

~

Minutes later, they emerged from the rocks and back out into the open mist. Whatever the origin of the green glow that permeated the realm, it was still farther beneath them.

Here, the species of fish became alien and otherworldly. A school of hand-sized fish passed, their bodies flat and swept back to thready fins like tassels trailing behind them; instead of shimmering in the green lights, their scales seemed to dissipate light—like dappled shadows in a forest. A huge angler fish passed like a lazy giant, its eyes and teeth demonically enormous; a lantern bulb hung from atop its head, blazing brilliantly, yet with the faintest silhouette of movement in the bulb.

Several times, the heroes and survivors stopped on the walkway and held their breath as something alien swam by them. Whether it was more timidness or awe, Helesys could not say.

A giant turtle passed by just at the edge of the misty light, so massive they could only see its lichen encrusted fins clearly while the rest of it passed like a ghost. Smaller fish clung to the sides of the great beast, holding on to its coarse skin with their faces while their bodies trailed behind them like worms.

Other creatures were too strange for the weaver to classify: There were clouds of immensely tiny creatures, the color of rust, and churning like a swarm of insects. Another group of creatures slipped by, their bodies ghostly white, thin and slender as ribbon—yet every few feet, Helesys saw tiny protrusions of fins. Another was little more than an enormous eye, nearly translucent, save for bright red veins. It drifted past whilst turning to watch them.

Despite their strangeness, all of the creatures passed without alarm, and all but the eye passed without acknowledging them—

Until the first mermaid appeared.

The first swam lazily into view. It had the torso of a Terran and the lower body of a fish—a body both slender and sexless, the entirety of it covered with sleek blue scales. Then it turned and stared directly at their group. Its eyes were large and black, like pools of void, and drifted from each Terran to the next. After its eyes drifted from Helesys, the weaver was drawn to the creature's hair—if it could be called such a thing. The strands drifted lazily about, more akin to jellyfish tentacles than the hair of a Terran.

Moments later, three more mermaids swam into view. Helesys turned to see more approaching from behind.

"Stay alert," Helesys said to the group, then she turned to the first mermaid, and called on her wand to translate. Her gauntlet hummed with energy and Helesys's voice became a mixture of clicks, groans, and squeaks. "*We mean you no harm.*"

The first mermaid drifted closer to the railing, its thin lips parting to speak. "*It has been long since a land-person has spoken our tongue. Longer still since one has swam with us.*"

*"We will not leave the railing,"* Helesys replied. *"We are continuing to the seam below."*

At that, the mermaid paused and shook its head. *"You will not get there by walking. Please, let us show you the way."*

Helesys's wand-arm thrummed with warning. *"We are staying on the platform. Get back."*

At this, the mermaids grew agitated, eliciting high pitched wines of distress. On the walkway, Taunauk and Shawn stood with weapons ready, glancing between the mermaids on either side.

*"You must let us help you,"* the mermaid wailed. *"There is no hope for land-people. You fall overboard and are cast off by the ships. You're always angry when you fall into our world, but in time you'll see. You always see. You long to be us. You struggle and fight, but when the breath leaves you, you find your place in the water with us."*

*"Get back,"* Helesys repeated, her metal arm humming with power. *"I won't ask again."*

The mermaid floated closer, her lithe hand reaching for Helesys's gauntlet.

The weaver shook her head, leveled her gauntlet, and fired. Crackling purple bolts erupted from her hand and tore the mermaid into chunks. Pieces were blown back and surged in the wake left by the blasts while red blood churned in the mist.

The other mermaids' wails of distress turned to hisses, and the creatures set upon them. The walkway became a maelstrom of fins, claws, blades, and arcane power.

Two more of the creatures as they lunged forward, pointed teeth bared, before Helesys blasted them. Meanwhile, Taunauk's axe and Shawn's knives slashed through half a dozen other mermaids in a blink. Somewhere in the turmoil were the silent gasps of the other Terran survivors as they huddled between the heroes and desperately clutched the railings.

A scream cut through the turmoil, and the weaver's blood ran cold. Helesys whipped around to see Scarlet's panicked face as the child was pulled under the railing by a mermaid. Isabella was frozen, both hands out, as if her body refused to acknowledge the child's absence.

"No!" Helesys screamed, but Scarlett was already gone. The creature held her close and dove into the abyss.

Helesys's mind reeled—churning power, bolstering her strength, and reaching for the jade lemur statuette in her pocket. Though the walkway was still leading them down and in the direction of the escaping mermaid, Helesys could never get past the other survivors on the crowded platform—she would have to fly.

But before Helesys could go after her, Shawn shouted, "I got her!" Then the rogue was over the side of the walkway and hurtling down into the mist.

Meanwhile, more of the shimmering mermaids swam through the veil of mist, appearing as quickly as their brethren were cut down.

Even on the narrow platform, the barbarian fought ferociously. Only an Endroggen could've wielded the massive battleaxe with such wide and wild arcs while minding the Terrans cowering at his back.

"To task!" Taunauk roared.

The barbarian's voice was faint, distant. Helesys's eyes flitted from target to target, her metal hand moving nearly as fast. Worry and doubt fell away, replaced by decisive violence. Dark power coalesced around her metal arm and spiraled away quicker than a breath—but not fast enough to stop the mermaids.

Helesys could've called on the Gar of Shéslang, but chose the Ring of Winter. She felt the horrible scraping along her nerves as the icy tendril of power slithered out from her ring finger.

"*Hieme murum*," she said, and the crystal ring glowed a brilliant blue.

Flakes of frost surrounded Helesys, and the icy tendril lashed out like lightning, flicking from mermaid to mermaid as they approached. The air around rose to a cacophony—the pained screams of the creatures, the sharp cracks of the frost whip, slices of Taunauk's blade, and the terror of the survivors huddled on the metal floor.

For those brief moments of chaos, mermaids fell like wilted pelts, split and bleeding. A dozen fell to the icy magic and a barbarian's blade, and the rest swam away in confusion.

Helesys ceased the winter magic and shivered at the return of the ring's tendril as it reached through her hand.

In the quiet, Isabella rose and peered into the abyss, looking for her daughter. She clasped her hands in front of her in silent prayer.

Meanwhile, Taunauk scanned the mist. As the moment passed, Helesys's gaze followed Isabella's, and as it dragged on, the weaver had to remind herself to breathe.

Soon they heard and felt footsteps echoing through the metal.

Shawn appeared, chest heaving and carrying Scarlett, who held tight around his neck. When he stopped, the girl turned around, leapt down and ran to her mother. Isabella looked her over and held her close.

At seeing the girl was unharmed, Helesys's concern changed to her comrade. Shawn's vest and shirt were soaked in blood.

Taunauk was first to ask, "Are you injured?"

Shawn glanced down and tried wiping away the blood—only succeeding in smearing it across the leather. "No, I'm fine. None of it's ours."

"That was foolish," Helesys said from the back of the group. "What happened to not jumping off?"

Shawn eyed her with a smile. "I don't take directions well. Besides, you looked like you were about to do the same thing. Glad I jumped first."

Taunauk asked, "How did you get back to the catwalk?"

The rogue reached into a pocket of his vest and pulled out a long black whip—something far too large for a normal pocket. "Apparently, I had this tucked away in my ethereal pouch."

~ ~ ~

# *Centrifuge*

In the aftermath of the mermaid attack, the group paused for a moment on the catwalk and talked quietly.

The barbarian wrinkled his face in question. "Is the whip magical?"

Shawn shook his head, absently holding the whip. "No. Of all the trinkets I've pulled out of there, that one isn't. But it was enough to reach the railing and pull myself and Scarlett out of freefall. As soon as we were near the catwalk again, gravity changed."

Though Scarlett still huddled with her mom in the middle of the survivors, the rogue looked refreshed by the theatrics of diving over the edge of the catwalk after the child.

In spite of the scene, Helesys felt herself drawn to questions. "What about swimming? Did you feel any different out there?"

"No," Shawn replied. "Whatever magic keeps the creatures suspended in the mist doesn't work on us." Then he made a gesture of falling accompanied by a quiet scream.

One of the men, a survivor, laughed. "That was... something," he said, voice trembling slightly.

Another said, "Are those things gone?"

Helesys looked to Taunauk and Shawn, unsure of how to answer. Shawn turned away and looked out into the mist, where strange behemoths were already swimming at the edge of view.

It was Taunauk that answered, forcing himself to stand up straight and stoic as he did. "*Those* creatures are gone, for now. There will be others. There always are. And that's what we are here for."

Helesys met young Scarlett's eyes and nodded, echoing Taunauk's certainty. There was no erasing the dread and danger that no doubt waited for them, no promising that the heroes could protect them—all of them. But Taunauk's words kindled the survivor's spirits against the cruel winds of the dungeon.

~

The heroes continued down the catwalk, the metal path taking them deeper and deeper into the eerie green space beneath the attic. Shawn led them into the green, followed by Helesys and the survivors, and Taunauk guarding their rear.

The number of great beasts that swam through the mist thinned until they were singular monsters so large that they only appeared as walls of mottled scales or fins larger than a ship's mainsail; their deep rumblings filled the air and rattled the catwalk. The heroes and survivors had passed from the realm of the strange to that of giants and titans.

Much of the journey passed in silence. After the mermaid attack, no one would chance drawing the curiosity of other creatures.

And still, they walked along the path until finally they were alone. Even the great beasts had their limits, it seemed, and the Terrans were left with only the metal echoing dully beneath their steps.

Sometime later—perhaps hours—a white wall emerged from the mist, and caused the entire group to stop. The metal platform and railings extended directly into it and ended.

It was several moments before anyone realized what they were staring at. Finally, Shawn said, "I think we've reached the floor."

As he and the group inched forward, the seams of large square tiles came into view. When they reached the end, Shawn slowly raised a foot forward toward the floor and felt for a change in gravity.

Shawn turned and grabbed hold of the railing as he reoriented himself. After a moment, he had fully shifted, and it appeared like he was standing on the wall. The rogue and Helesys helped the rest of the group complete the shift, and soon the entirety of them was standing on the white tile floor.

The green mist seemed to be thinner here on the ground than it had been in the upper reaches of the room, but it hadn't left completely. Helesys could only see a few hundred feet in front of them. Beyond that was hidden by the ominous green mist.

Helesys felt the pull of her wand-arm leading off into the unknown. "What does your coin say, Shawn?"

The rogue reached into his pocket and thumbed the coin, then pointed off in the same direction.

The weaver nodded. "At least we have that."

Again, the group resumed their order, now condensed into a circle rather than a line. They walked in silence for a few minutes before Shawn broke it.

"What happened back there with the mermaids?" he asked.

"The creature said it wanted to swim with us. To take us over the railing like it nearly took Scarlett."

The rogue shook his head. "Yep, every time you speak in tongues with some strange creature, it's never good.

Scarlett whispered from the middle of the clustered survivors, "How did you know, Helesys? How did you know we wouldn't be able to swim?"

"I didn't, not in so many words," the weaver replied quietly. "My wand warned me, and it has never been wrong. Strange creatures may resemble Terrans, but they are not Terrans. And it is a mistake to assume that they think the same way.

"Last death, we sailed aboard a ship and across waters at the edge of the realm. Along the way, we came upon an island. Thinking it safe harbor, we nearly stopped there. But there were strange Terrans there… They didn't speak to us, but sung to us from shore. Hypnotized us. Several men went to their deaths.

"They had looked innocent enough; they were anything but."

Silence fell again, settling in like mist between them.

Shawn motioned for Helesys to walk beside him, and she edged closer. "I saw you reaching for the jade lemur. Is it recharged yet?"

Helesys nodded. "I feel it. I nearly used it."

"Save it. We may need it. Besides, everyone's gotten used to walking." The rogue's words were solemn.

For a moment, their eyes met, and a grave understanding passed between them. If it came to that, the lemur would never carry all of them. Helesys wondered if it would ever carry three of them.

Then their eyes drifted back to the mist, both refusing to say what they were thinking.

Instead, Helesys spoke to something else as she watched the mist.

*Are you there, wand?*

*I am with you, always, Helesys Byyra.*

*I have questions.*

*I may have answers.*

Helesys asked, *In battle, sometimes the world feels distant. Is that you taking over? I have felt my metal arm move of its own accord before… before I knew that you were there.*

*There have been times, yes, that I have moved the metal without your knowledge or your direction. But the times you speak of are different. That is your training as a soldier. There are skills, maneuvers, and abilities that are so learned and ingrained in your psyche that you need not think of them. They are instinct to you—as natural as breathing.*

Helesys smiled bitterly, being sure to keep her face toward the fog and away from her allies. *So, that is why violence comes so easily to me.*

Her wand replied, *Did you ever doubt that? Your first memories were of blastshells. Taunauk once told you that your nature does not define you, and I echo those words now—you are more than just a soldier.*

Helesys looked to Taunauk, saw his steadfast vigil at the back of the group. He walked with Everfall and axe in hand, vigilantly searching the fog.

The weaver said inwardly, *Both you and the Endroggen are right, even if this elf is slow to believe it. This place has been a blessing, to see ourselves anew and without the coloring of memories. And a curse, to wonder what choices could've been different.*

Had others in the dungeon felt a similar sentiment? Perhaps most did not have the time between the confusion and terror, and the pain of death and rebirth. She could not deny that

Scarlett and Isabella would likely answer differently than One-Mind, Amadeus, or the Deacon. Regardless, Helesys regretted not asking others that question.

In the end, her wand was silent too as the weaver scanned the mist and pondered questions far beyond it.

She longed to be rid of this realm, and to find the God-peak—not just to reach the summit and find answers to her comrades' pasts, but to find relative safety. Then she resolved to talk with her friends.

~

As the heroes and survivors walked through the fog, it seemed as if time was blurred as well. Helesys couldn't say how long they had been walking, only that the mist began to swirl, as if wind or life had stirred it.

Wordlessly, Helesys, Taunauk, and Shawn drew their weapons and formed a circle around the survivors, who huddled together in the middle.

They waited. Helesys's wand-arm hummed with power and her breathing felt loud in her ears. Yet nothing came for them.

Finally, something appeared at the edges of the mist—

White walls. An enormous circular room surrounding them.

As they all glanced around, it was Shawn who first noticed the white ceiling above them.

"That's not good," the rogue mumbled.

Taunauk stepped several paces back the way they had come with shield and axe raised. Later, he called to them, "The way is gone. We are enclosed."

Helesys reached out with her wand and sensed magic building around them. Nothing so suffocating and blatant as the trap in the hall of the Idnauthi ship, but nefarious nonetheless. Like a bubbling kettle or the tense air before a storm.

The weaver held the Gar of Shéslang fast, and split her power between her gauntlet and her bolstered strength. Watching. Waiting.

In the distance, the farthest mist shuddered and began to spin—the whole of it moving to the right and building. The vortex built speed and spread inward until it swirled around their group.

Though Helesys felt the eerie cold whipping across her skin, she heard no sound, no wind.

The formless mist coalesced, forming thick lines.

A blob of mist grew in front of Helesys, close enough to touch, expanding up and down until it reached the white floor and was as tall as she was. Then the mist expanded and curved, forming a silhouette. Helesys watched as shoulders, a neck, arms, hips, and legs all appeared.

In the span of two breaths, Helesys was staring at a gray, Terran form.

Gasps of surprise sounded, and she was suddenly aware that similar shapes appeared in front of the other heroes and survivors—each misty shape mirroring the Terran before it.

Beyond the shape, the cloud had been fading from the room, coalescing into these new forms.

Taunauk shouted over the wind, "Helesys, blast the wall!"

The weaver raised her gauntlet and fired four quick shots, each formidable. Each purple blast sailed into the swirling mist and toward the wall—

Only to be swept off course. Each blast was pulled hard to the right, along with the mist. Four explosions echoed dully against four different sections of white wall.

Helesys grit her teeth and dredged power, flooding her metal arm with energy from the spear. This time the Gar of Shéslang rattled in her hand and the gauntlet rattled in her shoulder.

She let loose a single blast that tore across the mist—barely wavering in its fury—and slammed into the wall, splintering it—

And the wall disappeared to the right. Helesys watched as the cracked panel circled around them. The walls were spinning.

Helesys glanced from the white floor to the walls—their motion now clear from the intermittent appearance of the cracked panel.

"The walls are moving," she muttered.

Then, Helesys's silhouette opened its eyes and stared back at her. She watched with mounting horror as the mist's form became solid—*became Terran.*

Short white hair, pale skin. Leather armor. Metal arm.

When Helesys saw the identical gauntlet, she looked up and found her own face staring back. The doppelganger stared back—its eyes and skin rippled with a fine gray mist.

Gasps echoed from the other survivors, punctuated by Shawn saying, "Oh shit."

The next time Helesys raised her gauntlet, she aimed for her doppelganger.

It moved. Before Helesys could fire, the doppelganger swung and knocked her metal hand away.

Behind her, similar impacts sounded—dull sounds of fists against flesh. Helesys imagined her comrades facing down their own mirror images, but before she could so much as glance that way, her doppelganger turned its gauntlet at her. The struggles of her comrades fell away.

Helesys grasped her spear with both hands, bolstering her strength and speed, and leapt forward in attack—batting away the doppelganger's arm just as an arcane blast erupted and slammed into the ceiling.

As fast and as strong as Helesys was, her enemy was a mirror. It too bolstered its strength and speed, narrowing dodging swipes of the magical spear and blocking others with its own gauntlet. The weaver fought herself with a flurry, minding the errant, powerful blasts of her mirror's gauntlet and batting them away from her comrades.

Furious moments and a dozen strikes later, the mirror fainted left and Helesys had turned on her foe. Then she saw her comrade's struggle in earnest, if only for a moment:

Taunauk and his mirror grasped the axe between them, wrestling and kicking at one another. Everfall cast aside somewhere on the floor.

Shawn and his mirror were blurs of speed, little more than vacant afterimages.

The survivors were pure chaos. Each of the Terrans were wrestling with their own doppelgangers. Helesys could make out little, other than one man furiously holding onto a silver Scarlett whilst fighting his own mirror.

And in the fray, Helesys turned to their advantage: Aside from her gauntlet, the mirror images did not seem to have their weapons and heirlooms.

Helesys called on the Ring of Winter. Icy desolate power flowed into the Gar of Shéslang, so much that the temperature dropped around the pair and mist reappeared on their breath. She'd slain the Rithdai with such power, breaking through its immense armor plating.

The doppelganger raised its metal arm to block a strike, and the impact of the spear left heavy frost on its metal arm. The creature recoiled, eyes flaring wide and screeching—its voice like a metal blade scraping over stone.

Twice more, the creature tried to fire at Helesys. Each time, it was met with an icy impact of the spear and the blasts deflected up at the ceiling. The next blow shattered the doppelganger's metal arm. Icy pieces fell and smoldered into mist.

Helesys battered it again and again, the impacts rattling her shoulders and her teeth. Then she ran the screeching thing through the chest with the spear.

As it writhed beneath her, mist fuming from its mouth and its wound, Helesys looked back.

Behind her, her allies were still locked in terrifying struggles. Taunauk and Shawn's battles had strayed from the group, meanwhile the usual tight group of Terrans had broken, and each was struggling in their own separate purgatory of battle.

Taunauk was still trying to wrest the solitary axe from his mirror's hands, an Endroggen just as strong, ferocious, and filled with rage as Taunauk. Blood and mist dripped from their faces and chests where hilt or blade had struck in the frenzy.

Shawn and his mirror were both impossibly fast, both seeming as if they were made of mist. Even with her bolstered faculties, Helesys caught only the briefest glimpses of their fight.

The other Terrans's struggles were small in comparison but no less violent. Blood streamed from cut and busted faces. Hands wrapped around throats as they rolled around the ground.

Little Scarlett was on her back, beating furiously at her mirror's arms—for a moment it had been impossible to tell which was which, until Helesys saw the trails of fingernail marks on their faces. The girl on the ground was bleeding while the mirror straddled her and choked her.

Helesys twisted and wrenched the spear—still impaled in her doppelganger, and finally heard the horrid screech cease. Suddenly, the spear lurched, signalling that the creature had dissolved into mist.

Her eyes flitted from one battle to the next, pondering her options. She had many spells, but few that wouldn't indiscriminately harm her allies.

The weaver had once used the blight spell to kill woodsmen and recently to kill the young Idnauthi slugs. The spell sucked the water from both. Now, Helesys concentrated on the spell and bolstered it with the Gar of Shéslang.

*"Siccum putredine.."*

Mist erupted from her gauntlet and rolled like a wave toward the group and then over them.

Instantly, the doppelgangers shuddered and coughed—

The moment's lapse was enough for Taunauk to wrench the axe from his mirror's hand's. He slashed wildly, the first cleaving through the creature's arm at the shoulder, embedding in its ribs, and nearly knocking the mirror over. Mist billowed from its wounded arm and side. In an instant, Taunauk twisted, pulling the blade free, then swung again—the axe blade sunk deep into the creature's chest. The sound of crunching bone filled the air and the false Endroggen fell in a heap to the ground before melting completely into silver mist.

In the same instant, Shawn's enemy slowed; the blur became a wispy figure. The skin that had form was pale, parts of it oozing mist, while the leather armor seemed relatively intact. Helesys scarcely had time to see it because in the same instant it became visible, Shawn slammed into the back of the creature, twin daggers embedded in its back. The mirror was already dissolving, and the last glimpse Helesys saw of it was its eyes flashing a brilliant green and void dripping from its mouth.

Meanwhile, the other mirror creatures that accosted the rest of their group sputtered and faltered, but the other Terrans did not have the weapons that the heroes did. Taunauk and Shawn turned on the mirrors first, cleaving and slashing through several, while Helesys ran over to the group. She grabbed the last—the tiny, sputtering mirror of Scarlett—dropped the spear and pulled the creature off the girl. Then she spun round so that the child couldn't see and blasted the creature through the chest with her gauntlet. Helesys closed her eyes and dropped the lifeless creature. Instead of falling to the ground, it faded into mist.

Helesys turned to the group, all still save for their panicked breaths. It was several moments before the survivors huddled around each other again.

When Helesys was satisfied that everyone was alive, she turned back to the mist and the spinning white walls of the room—

But they were gone. There was nothing save for creeping mist around them, and the familiar veil of mist beyond that.

The room had vanished as suddenly as it had appeared.

~ ~ ~

# Crucible

"You've got to be kidding me," Shawn said, gesturing to the mist that surrounded them. "Where did the room go? How does—It just up and vanished. Just like that?"

Helesys ushered the other Terrans to their feet, and the ragged group looked to her, the weariness clouding their eyes. None of them gave breath to their concerns, but the weaver felt them, all the same.

Taunauk laid a hand on the rogue's shoulder. "To task," was all he said.

Taunauk picked up the Everfall shield from the ground, and Helesys picked up the Gar of Shéslang. Then the group continued into the mist, following the ever present trail of magic.

Shawn pulled out his magic coin and muttered, "There had better be some drink at the end of this journey, coin—*the alcoholic kind.*" He stared at the token, wide eyed for a moment, as if he expected a reply before finally placing it back in his pocket.

Helesys couldn't help but smirk at the display. "Do you really think there will be drink in this place?"

"A man's gotta have hope, doesn't he? I think we could all use it after what we've been through."

Helesys walked close to the rogue. "What was that back there? Right before your mirror died, its eyes were green and its mouth was black… Mine did not appear that way."

Shawn shook his head and continued to watch the mist as they walked. "It had my ears too: One elven and pointed, one human. *It was me*, Helesys. I don't know what to make of it." A moment passed before he continued. "When I was alone in the fishmens' realm, I ran into a creature that changed shape. I think it was something like those sirens we saw on the *Malorienta*. It changed into a similar shape. Its eyes were emerald green and its mouth was black…" Shawn trailed off, his brow wrinkled in thought or distress, though he tried to hide it.

"I do not know what that means for you," Helesys said, earnestly, "but a wise Endroggen once said that our past does not define us. We were all different people before we were trapped here. I imagine we will learn more about ourselves when we reach the Godpeak. What you do with that information is up to you."

Shawn shook his head again. "You don't have to do that. I'm not afraid. It's just—it's like looking in a mirror and remembering pieces of yourself long forgot."

"A *half-remembered life*," Helesys offered, recalling his poetry aboard the *Malorienta*. "Remember anymore poetry?"

Shawn smiled, something small but warm. "Tidbits. Isolated verses. Something about a vampyre, Bellasandra Liesl. Another about a rockman, Aukin Véo. Nursery rhymes…"

"So many. Would you share one?"

Shawn sighed, eyeing her reluctantly before turning away. *"The elves hold a secret in Novissimé, the city that scrapes the sky. Behind their walls of frosted glass, between clockwork gods and undying eyes.*

*"A realm happened upon fateful day and broken open to everlasting night.*

*"Where shadow walks and echoes of soldiers are cut down like wheat—soul discarded, sons and daughters incomplete.*

*"Bellum Aeternum. The steady pour of lives and ether. The war, the realm, become the flood."*

Helesys walked aimlessly as she listened, her gaze falling to the white floor, vaguely aware of her boots upon it. Her face twitched in surprise and shock.

*Bellum Aeternum*—the old words, the noble words, for The Eternal War.

Vague glimpses and memories came back to her: The sharp smell of ether, the sprawling cracked-glass desert, the sound of blastshells—

That familiar, gut-twisting fear as the explosions neared, and all went quiet.

"Helesys…" Shawn whispered. "I thought you would want to hear it."

She nodded slightly, forcing herself to breathe.

"Are you alright?"

The weaver nodded again, then added, "I liked your one about dreams better. Tell me a happy one next time."

Shawn eyed her a moment before turning back to the mist. "I will, when I remember one."

~

The group walked in silence, the featureless white floor and mist-veiled landscape drawing on so long that it seemed to taunt them.

Some time later, it seemed as if the floor ended completely—like they had come to the edge of an enormous cliff. Either end of it stretched off into the mist.

"It's like the edge of the godsdamn world," Shawn muttered as they approached.

It wasn't until they were close to the edge that they saw the realm continued. At the edge of the white floor, black ash sloped down and away from them.

She felt the silent urging of her wand, drawing them over the edge and ever deeper into the realm.

Helesys and the others exchanged wordless looks, then climbed over the edge.

They half-walked, half-slid down the powdery slope, their boots kicking up dust and forcing the lot of them to spread out wide. Taunauk and Shawn were at either end, where Helesys slid down the middle along with the unarmed Terrans.

Slowly, the mist thinned, revealing wider swathes of the desolate hillside.

They had slid for about an hour, and the mist was thin enough that they could see around them for a mile. Equally slow, the slope of the hill began to flatten.

The slope was faint when they saw the first glass tubes. They rose out of the ground in clusters of twelve, like bare, twisted bramble.

Throughout their journey down the slope, the survivors and the heroes had been hesitant to speak. Somehow, the silence had grown even more pronounced as they approached that cluster of piping. Each was a different size, the smallest a sword width, while the largest was enough for a Terran.

No one breathed as liquids began to bubble up through the thinnest tubes, followed by bones and organs. Then clothes and skin.

Helesys tried to think of the direction they had come—if they had double-backed somehow and come to the same sets of piping as they had passed so far above on the catwalk. But the weaver found it unlikely.

When the parade of entrails was done, the cluster of pipes shook and then writhed like lazy, hanging snakes. They undulated and slithered through black ash and away from the group, leaving a wake in the sand.

They watched in muted horror for several minutes as it wriggled away. Until it was several hundred feet away and stopped, then began sucking up more Terran pieces from somewhere under the ash.

Quiet mutterings rose from the survivors.

Helesys turned to them. "We're nearly there," she said softly, trying to quiet them. Her words were meager and helped little, but they were better than silence.

~

They saw several more clusters of glass tubes in the distance, wavering like snakes. Wherever they were going, the mist continued to clear and the glass became more numerous. Like the ends of a grisly black desert.

At the edges of the mist, Helesys could see the slope curving around on itself, and it called to mind the image of an enormous crater. Her wand and Shawn's coin seemed to be leading them right to the epicenter.

Pools of liquid appeared on the slope, clear with tinges of silver and white. Though the slope of the crater had lessened, it was still noticeable; the pools clung to the ash, defying gravity. Mist simmered from them.

As the group paused, Shawn continued walking forward, magic coin in hand.

He was nearly upon the nearest small pool, when Taunauk said, "That is not wise."

Shawn waved a dismissive hand, peered down at the silvery puddle, then waved away the mist.

"Godsdamnit," the rogue muttered. "*Sorry.*"

"You don't have to apologize," Helesys replied. "We're going the right way."

But Shawn turned, eyes wide. "You heard that?"

"Heard what?" she replied.

From behind her, Scarlett said, "I heard it. The other voice."

Now all eyes were on the rogue as he held out the coin. "It doesn't just lead to drink. *It talks.*" But as he stared intensely at it, only silence followed. "I said, *it talks…* Alright, well it apologizes for always being wrong… And it laughs at a joke now and then—you can stop looking at me like that." Shawn shoved the coin back in his pocket. "Well, there's no way I'm drinking *that*. Helesys, I guess we're following you now."

Helesys laid a reassuring hand on his shoulder. "We're still going the right way."

Then she led the group, while Shawn walked with the survivors and Taunauk followed at the rear.

From behind her came Scarlett's voice again. "I really did hear it, Mr. Shawn."

"Thanks, kid."

Up front, Helesys smiled, the expression all but hidden from her comrades.

~

Sometime later, Helesys's wand said, *I heard the coin.*

Helesys asked inwardly, *Why didn't you speak up? Shawn shouldn't think himself crazy.*

*It wouldn't have done any good.*

*What do you mean?*

*Not all magic items speak as I do. Shawn should not expect his coin to reply. Rather, it's a marvel that it replies at all.*

Helesys looked out over the ashen crater and growing number of puddles. Inwardly, she said, *Please explain why.*

*Most magic items are not sentient, in a living sense. They are merely concentrated and focused magic, no different than a sword, a chain link, or a horseshoe. They are all made for a purpose, sometimes only to embody a single spell. Shawn's knives, for instance, are each made to target a weakness. Shawn's coin leads to a mind-altering drink like liquor.*

*Then what are you made for?*

*To both cast and counters a vast number of spells.*

I take it that makes you rare, for a wand.

*Yes.*

*What did I do to deserve such a boon?*

*You were an exceptional soldier, Helesys Byyra. The power of an artifact is limited by the bearer. Only an equally skilled mage could use so many spells to their full potential.*

Helesys frowned and asked, *It would behoove the elves to keep such a powerful weapon on The Eternal Battlefield… Why was I permitted to leave? And to leave with you?*

*I do not know. But I do know that it would not be easy to separate us. The connections between the wand and your gauntlet are intricate, like clockwork. They would've required great skill and time to separate. Your gauntlet is of similar complexity.*

Her wand continued, *You were a member of Great House Byyra. Injured in The Eternal War, and given both a new arm and a new weapon with which to fight. You must have been given an important mission, one that led you outside Novissimé.*

*Or I ran away,* Helesys thought.

A moment later, her wand replied, *That is another possibility.*

Helesys nodded to herself. She would've given much just to have the answers.

The dungeon seemed built on suffering and endless death. But there was also the theft of their memories, and at times Helesys could not decide which was worse.

Even if her earliest worries were true—that Helesys would not have liked her past self, that she was an adept soldier, but also cold and ruthless—she would rather have known the truth.

"Are we close, Helesys?" Taunauk's voice came suddenly from the back of the group, startling her.

All at once, she was brought back to ashen slopes—to the dungeon. Helesys felt the direction of her wand, the feeling subtle yet growing, directing them ever deeper into the crater. But the wand's voice was silent, slipped somewhere back into the ether, into some space between.

It seemed that each time Helesys spoke to her wand, the immediacy of the world fell away.

"We're close," the weaver finally said, "but we still have a ways to go."

Helesys had so many questions, and every time she found an answer, it only succeeded in raising more questions.

As they walked, the landscape was still changing: The slope of the crater was nearly gone. Puddles of liquid mist were both larger and more numerous, looking like islands in a black sea. And the glass tubes had changed too—

New structures formed around the bases of the outcroppings of glass: Shiny, red and white growths that climbed up the sides of the tubes. At first, they were no more than a foot high, tapering as they reached up the glass tubes, but as the clusters of tubes grew more numerous, they grew larger. Again Helesys thought of desert giving way to a forest, and of shrubs and trees growing denser.

Helesys motioned for the group to wait as she investigated one of the strange structures. Kindling strength, she walked closer enough to touch it. On this particular thing, the red and white material was as tall as she was. The base of it had grown bulbous, like over-ripened fruit, and it pulsed softly as if it were alive. Up close, she could see that the glistening surface wasn't wet, but rather semi-translucent, like the glass that rose up out of it. It smelled of metal and blood.

~

Soon the strange outcroppings reached twice as tall as Helesys, and their forms grew ever stranger. At first, it looked as if they might be adapting a plant-like shape, with leaves and blossoms jutting off of the bulbous center structure. But instead of leaves, the projections grew into abstract, branching shapes—like mineral deposits in a cave.

The mists had all but vanished, but were visible above as distant clouds tainted with green. The heroes had walked to the ends of the obscurity and the vast expanse of the crater was laid bare.

Ahead of them, the structures grew wider and higher, creating archways between the glass tubes that rose up into the clouds.

In the distance, a pink crystalline spire rose up into the clouds, piercing the heavens.

Helesys had stopped in a small clearing and was staring at the distant monument, when Taunauk stood beside her.

"Is that it?" the Endroggen asked quietly.

Helesys nodded.

He grunted in response.

"Taunauk, what in Movernus's name is this place?" she asked. "It's a crater but…"

"A wound in the realm. Blackened sands. Scabbing over in places."

Helesys looked upon the realm anew and saw that he spoke the truth. Somehow, she *felt* it.

"What of the glass?"

Taunauk sighed and eyed the skyline of tubes. "Something unholy. We should not linger here."

From behind them, Shawn said, "To task!"

But even the rogue's jest couldn't lighten the mood. Taunauk was right. The sense of dread was only increasing as they walked further into the crater, like they were wandering close to the edge of a cliff again, like the world might suddenly drop out from beneath them.

~

The unholy trees grew higher still, their pink branches twisting around the glass tubes like creeping vines and flaring out across the sky—a ghastly forest canopy or the roof of a shattered cathedral.

And the tops of the trees began to writhe, shudders spreading across the woven branches, though Helesys felt no wind.

To their right, a white and red trunk squirmed, the long muscles rearranging themselves into a ring.

Helesys paused and the eyes of the group fell upon it.

Inside the ring, slivers of flesh became the abstract lines of eyes and a mouth. The flesh of the trunk bulged, a motion that made the face appear as if it was looking at each of their group in turn before settling on a point in their center.

It spoke, mouth unmoving, its voice like the crunch of glass and bone, seeming to echo from the entire tree. "You are not Sigun." It spoke the common tongue.

Helesys stood at the front of the group, and so she replied, "We are travelers, seeking a seam."

The face ignored her. "Sigun brought me subjects… You do not look ready. Tell Sigun that I expected more from our mutual research."

Helesys chose her words carefully. "We will not see Sigun before we leave the seam."

"Beautiful creatures, Idnauthi. I longed for the privilege to assimilate them."

Someone behind her grumbled uneasily.

The weaver asked, "What is your name?"

"This is merely an extension of Mr. Mask."

"Then Mr. Mask, we need to leave this realm and will do so by traveling the seam."

"I'm afraid that is impossible in your current state. You will require assistance."

Helesys struggled to keep her voice flat. "What is wrong with the realm?"

"It is not the realm," the face in the tree replied. "You are not ready. I will be with you, shortly."

The muscles of the face relaxed, the lengths of them seemingly to slither back into the tree itself, and the face was gone.

The single sky-piercing tower in the distance began to shake, and something akin to skin sloughed from its surface, leaving blood-laced crystal behind.

And as that pink skin reached the lower towers, it reshaped into spindly limbs and strode across the ghastly landscape like some slender yet titanic spider.

Then the ground and the twisted towers shook.

"Mother of Movernus," Shawn said.

"Gods, what do we do?" one of the surviving men said.

Behind her, Helesys was vaguely aware of her comrades drawing their arms and the survivors huddling together, the latter barely held fast by panic.

But she couldn't take her eyes off of the monstrosity lumbering across the sky.

She felt the sudden alarm of her wand, and was already kindling power, heart beating in her throat. Her mind reeled, and the weaver turned over possibilities in her mind. So little would affect something that monstrous. Last, she patted the pocket of her vest, and felt the small comfort of the jade lemur—should they have no other choice.

"Be ready," Taunauk said, but his voice grew quiet as the rumbling grew louder.

In moments it was upon them. The trees and structures were groaning beneath its weight. It strode until its midsection towered above them, blotting out the green cloud.

It towered over them, its thin mottled limbs the same twisted flesh as the trees beneath. It looked as if the sky had been torn open and its bloody rib cage hung above them.

The skin of its underside writhed, fibrous tissue coiling and slithering into the outline of a face. And when it spoke, its voice came from all around them with creak of bone and whine of glass.

"You who have rejected the Idnauthi, do not despair. You are one of many. Here, the fortunate shall find death. Those who resist shall find their place among the snow, the chaff, and broken glass."

When the thunderous voice ended, the trees around them began to split and tear. Mist seeped from the trees around them and from each came a wispy Terran outline. Then flesh oozed from the tree followed after, following the outline of the mist like a grisly afterimage.

Helesys watched the nearest of these creatures step forward. It was nearly Helesys's height, and she watched the flesh shape itself into a feminine face and long pink strands of hair. Dress lines appeared across the shoulders and the sinuous lines of flesh, smoothened into lines of fabric.

From the outline alone, the elf felt a pang of familiarity. She had seen the dress before… and as its ears grew to elven points, Helesys's mouth parted in horror.

And colors began to flash overtop the grisly visage, like shadows flickering in the firelight. The perfect image of Helesys's mother alternating with her sister and the skinless creature like a grisly flipbook.

Behind her, similar expressions of fear and surprise rang out.

Helesys gripped the Gar of Shéslang tight with both hands and called upon magical power. It didn't matter what grisly weapons were brought against her. She was ready to smash it in one decisive blow, to be rid of it, and hoped the others would do the same.

"Helesys, why did you leave?"

Wynbella's voice—her mother's voice—came from the creature, clear as a memory. And as it spoke, the grisly flipbook stopped, and Helesys looked upon the perfect image of her mother. Long white hair cascading over her evening gown.

The emblazoned *B* for House Byyra. Smile smiled warmly, but her eyes betrayed her; it was a bittersweet smile.

Helesys flinched and her heart began to race.

"We've missed you so. Come back home where you belong," Wynbella said.

In spite of kindled power, in spite of her wand rattling with warning, Helesys took a step closer to her mother.

"You don't have to fight anymore. You've sacrificed enough, haven't you?" Wynbella said, gesturing toward the metal arm.

Then her mother's visage changed to Aradi, her sister. Her smile twisted to a scowl.

"Yes. Come back, Helesys. Fail at another mission. This is just one more thing you can't do right."

Momentary joy at seeing Aradi was erased, leaving Helesys feeling as if she'd been punched in the gut. The weaver's face became a mirror.

"You lie," Helesys sneered. "You *always* lie!" And in that moment, she spoke as much to the memory as she did to the creature beneath it.

The warning of her wand became a pulse in her ears, and the weaver lashed out with bolstered strength. The spear slammed down across the shoulder of Aradi—she crumpled to the ground with the sound of crunching glass.

Helesys held the spear close, hands trembling.

She whipped around to see all the group facing similar memories: The surviving Terrans reached hesitantly out to the visages gathered around them. Shawn knelt down, reaching out to a young, soot-covered boy. Taunauk stood in front of an older Endroggen man—the side of his face glistening with tears.

"They are lying!" Helesys shouted, but the others stared and pleaded with the creatures.

The weaver raised her gauntlet at the child—the creature—in front of Shawn, meaning to blow it away.

A hand seized her arm, and the blast careened into the bloody trees. Red powder burst from the wound. Wynbella clutched Helesys's metal arm, her eyes pleading, neck lurched to one side.

"Come back to me, Helesys—"

But the visage had already changed to the snarling visage of Aradi. "Why are you struggling—did you change your mind again? Want to come back and be a princess?"

Helesys wrenched her arm, turning the palm so it was flat against the creature's chest. Aradi didn't let go. Didn't even try to move away from the charging blast.

"You can't even die right," Aradi sneered.

There was a wet thump of impact, and the visage of Aradi flickered again, turning back into the grisly flipbook of mother, sister, and creature. Its grip went slack and the two halves of it that were left fell in a heap to the ground.

Helesys pushed thoughts away and turned to face the others. One by one, she leveled her gauntlet at them and let power fly. Screams rang out as memories were brutalized before their eyes.

Taunauk turned first, bringing his axe down upon two of the closest monstrosities—completing the grisly ritual.

In the confusion, Taunauk and Shawn turned to her, tears streaking their face like war paint—mirroring her own.

The split flesh on the ground began to writhe, pieces of crippled memories flickering all around them.

From within came the quiet voice of her wand-arm: *We must run.*

Helesys grit her teeth and craned her head at the titan looming above. The turmoil brought on by seeing her mother and sister fumed within her.

*Helesys, we must run.*

The others circled together, Taunauk and Shawn at the ready.

Instead, the weaver reached out with her power, feeling the blistered melding of flesh and thing. She followed the trees wrapped around the glass tubes, and followed the flesh that stretched across the landscape like a spider's web. She traced up the monstrosity, following its legs to the face hanging in the sky.

*"Do you feel them in there, Helesys?"* Shawn's voice. Moments later, she realized was hearing his voice inside her head. *"They're in there. So many… Sleeping—dormant."*

She stared up at Mr. Mask, as she peered into its mind. Inside, she felt a well of souls as vast as the star-filled sky. In so many ways, the bleeding city reminded her of the hellscape of the parasite city of the *Duoausongur*, but where the parasite's voice was only one—only of hunger—Mr. Mask's realm was millions.

She felt the titan gaze back. The voice of legion echoed through the weaver's mind. *"You call me a liar, and you turn away from the truth?"*

It felt as if the stars had fallen to the ground and screamed in a cacophony all around her. They were the blistered trees and the bleeding city.

Helesys's mind swam, and In desperation, she dredged power—drawing on it as if she were drowning in the souls around her. Thoughts of water, thoughts of mist—

For a moment, she was back in the Apothecary's study as the witch turned herself to smoke. Was it really so different

now? Each soul like a drop of water. Mr. Mask was not one—
it was many.

Because she had nothing else in the face of oblivion, the
weaver concentrated on the souls. The power that nearly killed
the Apothecary rattled in her metal arm, then Helesys com-
pounded it with the Gar of Shéslang—the spear that had
pierced the god serpent.

"*Amplificare potentia!*"

She released the power, and a shockwave burst forth that
quaked the ground and shook the trees. The entire realm shuddered.

The screams of millions of souls rang in Helesys's ears, and
somewhere, lost in the sea, was her own. The flesh of the trees
and the twisted landscape writhed as the many souls began to
fight for control. Above them, the twisted titan's skin bubbled
and frothed, and the weaver's vision began to blur.

Somewhere in the fray came the exasperated voice of
Shawn. "Holy shit! Run!"

Helesys felt someone grab her under the arm and pull her
up and running. Instinctively, she ran, following the group
while her vision swam.

In the distance, Helesys felt the seam of the realm. She
yelled and pointed toward it, her voice lost, hoping that her
comrades would understand her meaning.

~ ~ ~

# *Fluctuation*

As they ran, Helesys saw glimpses of the writhing land-scape—

But it felt so very far away.

With her magic blast, she'd given power to the millions of souls that lived in the grotesque landscape. With their new-found strength they had pulled Mr. Mad down from control and drowned him in the screams—now the souls scrambled over one another, desperate to climb higher. Each swearing never again to be trampled and voiceless. The realm was boiling.

It was like she'd set fire to the world. And Helesys felt lost in it.

"She sure picked a good time to go helpless," Shawn muttered. She barely heard.

Helesys tried to look at him, but she saw nothing except turmoil. Blistered trees squirmed and bleeding city quaked. Archways fell and shattered. Towers groaned before bursting and falling in a hail of frozen shards.

When One-Mind repaired the connection in her wand-arm, it warned her to be careful when using her wand to its full potential. For every spell she used, there was recoil—whether physical or psychic, or something else… This time it felt as if she'd held a blastshell in her hand, and nearly killed herself in the process.

"To task, Helesys." Taunauk's voice. Someone jostled her.

"Come on, weaver. We need you back here." Shawn…

Her head rolled back, and behind them the titanic spider was crumbling. It was falling in slivers and chunks of red—the backbone of the sky was collapsing.

And beyond, the sky was black as night.

In her mind, in the furthest reaches of the sky, Helesys saw creatures running along threads of metal—soulless things—faceless things—free from the confines of the attic and storming down the catwalks. Without the green light to stop them, they would overtake the realm. They poured forth like a plague.

"They're coming," Helesys muttered, eyes wide.

The world was coming back to her, a world of turmoil and panicked running. Structures around them had grown thick, and moments later, the group ducked into a bleeding building and ran down passages. The walls around them looked like cracked glass with threads of blood running through them.

"What did she say?" one of the survivors asked.

"They're coming," Helesys said again.

The world felt sharper now, no longer a blur. The smell of salt and metal overcame her. Their footsteps echoed through the halls.

She was suddenly aware of Taunauk holding under her arm, half propping her up, half dragging her.

"I'm fine now, Taunauk," she said, her feet stuttering only slightly.

The group slowed while the weaver's mind fully came back to the task of running. For a moment, she was confused why they weren't running at a superhuman pace—but she remembered the other Terrans in tow.

"Who's coming?" someone behind her asked.

"The faceless creatures," Helesys replied without looking back. "The seam is at the center tower."

"We're nearly there," the barbarian said.

"Good," Helesys replied.

They didn't have much time. She could feel the seam closing.

~

The heroes and survivors were completely inside the blistered structure, and the lightless sky was gone. All around them, walls of blood and grass spasmed with the rhythm of a dying heart.

Hallways twisted and turned, becoming a labyrinth the closer they got to the center—to the seam.

Helesys took to blasting through walls instead of navigating the maze. Her strength was back, and it was an easy thing to summon such familiar violence.

She blasted through the final wall, and beyond lay a vast open room. The floor was circular, some two hundred feet across, but the walls rose up to a point, to a spire, some impossible distance in the sky.

The entire floor was covered in geometric designs and runes in languages that Helesys didn't recognize, and she didn't have the time to decipher.

She led the group to the center and reached out for the seam. It was faint now—even with the gift of One-Mind and the Gar of Shéslang; the seam was fading and her grip was tenuous.

So concentrated was Helesys, that she barely noticed the muffled sound of rain echoing through the roof.

The group whispered in confusion, and moments later came Taunauk's voice.

"That's not rain. By the forgotten gods… Helesys, the warding light—Helesys!"

The weaver heard, and a breath later, light filled the room. The world was still around her, save for the abnormal pulsing of the walls—veins in the glass glowed a sharp pink in the harsh light.

The others huddled around Helesys, Shawn and Taunauk at the front, blades drawn. Beyond them were hundreds of faceless Terrans, standing just at the edge of the light. Some shuffled backward like lazy marionettes, but more of them filled the passages beyond—everywhere the weaver turned and as far as she could see.

A chill ran down her spine at how close they had come to being overrun by them.

Rain still sounded from the roof—the sound of faceless pouring out of the attic.

She kindled the warding light and reached back toward the seam. She needed to be quick, not just to escape but so that they didn't draw the ire of another being like Sigun or the Idnauthi.

A realm of frost whispered to her, of glaciers and a single mountain that rose so high it pierced the false heavens. Helesys seized this, then opened it for her comrades.

Chill air spilled through into the blistered tower, and the weaver ushered the survivors, the barbarian, and the rogue through.

Helesys was last, and she turned back at the faceless mass one last time. She looked for Sigun, that bastard Idnauthi, and cursed him—

The creatures turned from her to the walls of blood and glass, and stared at them. Then they pawed at the walls, scratching bleeding chunks out, staring at them and then casting them aside. Helesys was struck by the feeling that they were looking for something, perhaps for some part of them that was taken from them, a part that still lurked inside Mr. Mask or inside the horrid landscape the titan had made.

Helesys didn't find Sigun in the crowd. Her curse fell on deaf ears.

She stepped through the portal, leaving the crumbling realm of bodies and glass behind.

~

They emerged from the portal on a frigid plane. Icy snow crunched beneath their feet.

Helesys looked around and found that they were in the familiar starting room and hall, except that heavy snow had drifted in.

The wind came intermittently, and bit at their skin.

Beyond the room, the normally long hallway was cut short, as if the structure had been cleaved through. The end was now only a couple dozen feet away, and gave way to the snowy hillside, lit by bright moonlight.

Taunauk stood near the entrance, cloak pulled around him and peering out into the distance. Shawn and the rest of the group huddled together, hoping that their body heat would make up for the meager rags they wore for clothes.

Helesys shivered and turned her magic to task. She reached inward and turned her magic to bolstering her allies and herself. She had never used it in such a manner, but it felt a natural extension.

She felt the chill of the wind lessen until it was little more than a cool summer breeze. And she smiled as expressions of surprise and amazement spread across the faces of the others.

Shawn looked directly at her, already knowing what she had done, and returned her smile. "I think that's the best trick yet," he said. She remembered the rogue's pain even being near the freezing power of the Ring of Winter and hoped her spell would be enough for him.

But it was young Scarlett's smile that lifted the weaver. After all they had seen and lived through, the young elf dropped to her knees, grasped for the snow and marveled at it.

Moments later, Scarlett had fashioned it into a snowball and threw it at the weaver.

Helesys turned and the snow hit her in the shoulder, icy flecks falling down her collar. She smirked and grasped a handful of snow from the ground. Chaos ensued as the others joined in, and the room became a maelstrom of snowballs, melting the fear and the tension they carried.

Sometime later, Helesys saw Taunauk standing stoically in the hall. From the tracks in the hall, it looked as if he'd wandered to the end and back.

He stood, arms folded, dodging errant snowballs when they came his way. He smiled but never threw one back.

When their fervor finally slowed, Taunauk called to them. "It looks like there is a village down the hill, and the Godpeak is in the distance."

~ ~ ~

NEXT TIME ON
*A BATTLEAXE AND
A METAL ARM*
Book 12:


*A Promise of Winter*
Available March 2022

# Spoiler–Free excerpt from *BAMA 12*

They set toward the village first. Only Helesys, Taunauk, and Shawn were willing to make the journey up the Godpeak.

The weaver was glad for that, for it was a miracle that they'd been able to protect the survivors of the Idnauthi ship for so long. As much as Helesys would protect them, she was ready to leave them somewhere safe.

Helesys's wand kept the group warm, kindling their own innate fortitude or warmth. In spite of their meager clothing, they suffered the gales as if they were a cool Spring breeze.

But splitting her magic in so many directions was tricky. As powerful as her wand was, even it had limits. Helesys chuckled at this—that concentrating on such a mundane task should trouble her wand so, when it could bring such potent—even catastrophic—power to bear at other times.

*We are made for different things*, the wand whispered to her. *You and I were made to be weapons, not fireplaces.*

Helesys replied, *Maybe in our next life we will be so lucky. To live as something quiet and mundane.*

*Perhaps for you. If I were just a mundane wand, I would not exist.*

Helesys smiled, then turned to her comrades.

She walked in toward the middle and the right of the group. Taunauk led, and Shawn followed close behind.

No one talked—the wind was far too loud to keep up a conversation. And Helesys found herself glancing back intermittently toward the rogue.

Shawn met her eyes twice when she did this, both times giving her an animated thumbs up.

Still, she worried about Shawn. Though he had his own powers, he seemed sensitive to cold. In spite of magic warmth, she saw him rub his arms as if fighting off a chill.

# To be continued March 2022

# Thank you for Reading

I hope you enjoyed reading this story as much as I enjoyed writing it.

If you did, I would massively appreciate a short review on Amazon or your favorite book website. Reviews are crucial for any author, and a starred review or even just a line or two can make a huge difference.

It's especially true for the start of a series. Thanks and I hope you enjoy the next one!

# Looking for more Engrossing Fantasy?

You might like **Tales from Another World,** an ongoing short story series containing stories about sorcerers, druids, mortals, gods, thieves, and all other manner of Terrans.

The 2<sup>nd</sup> and 3<sup>rd</sup> installments are out and they tie into the outside world of *A Battleaxe and a Metal Arm.* So, if you're looking for more engrossing fantasy stories, and if you want to know more about this fantasy universe, read on and see how deep the rabbit hole goes.

# What questions do you have about *A Battleaxe and a Metal Arm*?

If you've read this far, hopefully you'll read a bit further—both in this book and across the series. I'm not sure how most authors write serials and how much of it is flying by the seat of their pants, but that's not how I do things. For all the major questions that might come up in BAMA, I already have answers for 95% of them. Same goes for the major plot points, twists and climaxes. That might sound boring to some, especially some of you other authors who enjoy variations of writing into the dark, but I think having a solid blueprint is paramount to writing a long series.

So, what questions do you have about the story? Here are a few:

1) ~~What is the dungeon?~~ It's a soul trap of overwhelming size and power. But where did it come from? Is it a force of nature or an ill-made weapon, or perhaps something else entirely? In the real world, it looks like a giant cloud with faces writhing just beneath the surface. Helesys speculates that the

reason no one remembers it is because it's so horrific their minds blot it out!

2) Who were Helesys and Taunauk before they got trapped? We've learned that Helesys was both a soldier and might have been elven royalty. Taunauk was an outlander either outcast or sent on some kind of a quest. How well did they know each other beforehand?

3) How did Helesys get her metal arm? Likely through injury, amputation, and replacement. She was likely fighting in the Eternal War, the war of the Elves against the Shadowkind.

4) Who is Shawn? Why does he feel so familiar to Helesys and Taunauk? The group speculates that they were traveling together for unknown reasons. Shawn worries that they were tracking him. This could explain why Helesys and Taunauk are always reborn together, while Shawn was usually alone.

5) Who is the Wolf King and what sinister plans does he have for our heroes? How did he come to rule over the Dungeon? How does the Gatekeeper factor into all this?

6) Who is the mysterious voice encountered on the white sandy shores of Meridian? Why do they seek the death of the Wolf-King? …And why did they choose the heroes?

Did I miss any questions? Probably. Connect with me and other *BAMA* fans on social media and compare questions!

I've got plans. I've got answers. And I've got them on a drip-feed. Keep reading and expect to find out a little more to the mysteries with each installment. Hopefully, you're as excited about this series as I am.

# Connect with the Author

If you want to stay up to date on the latest about Samuel's publishing news and blog, check out his website and consider signing up for his monthly newsletter.

www.SamuelFlemingBooks.com

Samuel can also be found on Reddit, Goodreads and Facebook.

Samuel Fleming is a Science Fiction and Fantasy author.

He grew up in Maryland, spending most of his time swimming and writing. Swimming gave him a lot of time to daydream, so the two hobbies complemented each other well. Idle day dreams turned into stories, some of which stuck with him for years. These days he swims a little less and writes a lot more.

He loves a good story no matter the medium: Books, TV, video games, comics, tabletop RPG's, or podcasts–most of which he attempts to share with his wife and three kids, and occasionally on his blog.